DEDICATED TO SUNNY, SHEPHERD, NEAL,
AND FOR EVERY CHILD THAT FEELS DIFFERENT.
BEING ONE OF A KIND...DOESN'T MEAN YOU'RE ALONE.

FIRST EDITION

LUNAR YARNS PUBLISHING

LUNAR YARNS PUBLISHING LLC

SPECIAL THANKS TO NATIONAL GEOGRAPHIC AND PAUL NICKLEN FOR PHOTOGRAPHY.
©PAUL NICKLEN/NATIONAL GEOGRAPHIC CREATIVE

PHOTOGRAPHY OF PAINTINGS BY KAREY RINKENBERGER
ISBN: 978-0-692-85042-8
LIBRARY OF CONGRESS CONTROL NUMBER: 2017902906
PRINTED IN THE UNITED STATES OF AMERICA

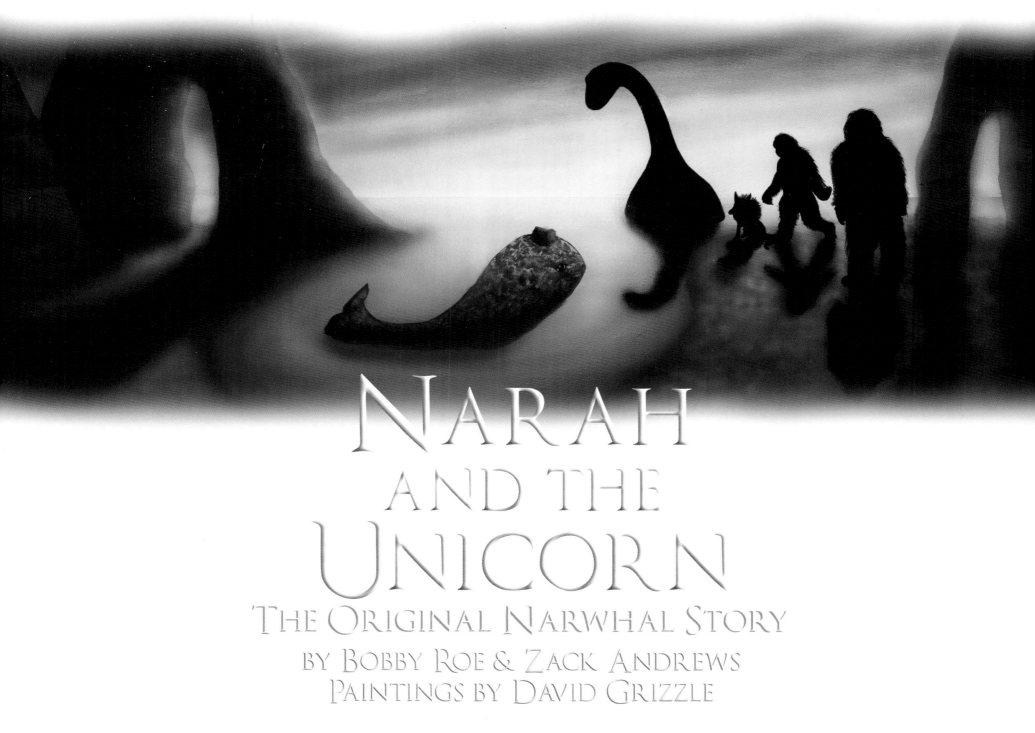

NARAH
AND THE
UNICORN
THE ORIGINAL NARWHAL STORY
BY BOBBY ROE & ZACK ANDREWS
PAINTINGS BY DAVID GRIZZLE

IN AN OCEAN NOT TOO FAR AWAY,
SWAM A WHALE NAMED NARAH. SHE WAS BORN WITH A
BARNACLE ON HER FOREHEAD AND NEVER HAD ANY FRIENDS.
THE OTHER SEA ANIMALS ALWAYS TEASED HER.

THEY CALLED HER BARNACLE BELUGA.

ONE DAY, NARAH SAW THE SILHOUETTE OF A
PECULIAR CREATURE SWIMMING JUST ABOVE HER.
EAGER FOR FRIENDS SHE SURFACED TO MEET HIM.

Hello, I'm Narah the Whale," said Narah.

The Unicorn replied, "Good day, I'm Peg the Unicorn."

"I've never met a Unicorn before," Narah curiously stated.
"As far as I know, I'm the only one of my kind.
We like it that way," Peg proudly told her.

"We?" Narah questioned.
"Well, I have some other friends that are unique like you," Peg whispered with a smile.

"I'm not unique. I'm strange to other Whales," said Narah.
"Be proud of being different. Why would you want to look like everyone else?
You're one of a kind, like me," Peg exclaimed.

THAT WAS THE BEGINNING OF A GREAT FRIENDSHIP.
NARAH AND PEG PLAYED TOGETHER EVERYDAY FOR YEARS.

SHE RACED AGAINST HIM IN THE SEA,

WHILE HE GALLOPED IN THE SAND.

EACH SUNSET, AFTER THEIR DAILY ADVENTURES,
NARAH WOULD BLOW MIST IN THE AIR
TO SAY GOODNIGHT. THE WATER CREATED A
BEAUTIFUL RAINBOW PRISM IN THE SKY.

THEN ONE DAY, PEG'S TIME ON EARTH
HAD COME TO AN END. A THOUSAND
YEARS FINALLY CAUGHT UP TO HIM.
HE GREW VERY WEAK.

NARAH SHED SO MANY TEARS,
THAT THE OCEANS ROSE THAT DAY.

WITH ONLY A COUPLE BREATHS LEFT,
PEG WHISPERED SOMETHING SPECIAL TO NARAH...

THEN HE REMOVED HIS HORN AND GAVE IT TO HER.

As the sun dissolved into the sea,
Narah wanted to honor Peg.

Several of his long lost friends attended.
There was...

NESSY, CHUPA, SQUATCHY AND YETI.

Narah struggled not to cry as she said Goodbye.

"Peg taught me a lot about life, friendship,
and that we are all God's creatures.
But the biggest lesson of all,
I want to share with you today."

"Why be a Gorilla...
when you can be Big Foot?
Why be a Polar Bear...
when you can be the Abominable Snowman?
Why be a Dog...
when you can be the Chupacabra?
Why be a Dinosaur...
when you can be the Loch Ness Monster?"

THEN NARAH SWAM AS DEEP AS SHE COULD
TO PUT PEG'S HORN IN A SAFE PLACE.

SHE HID IT IN A TREASURE CHEST
THEY FOUND ON ONE OF THEIR ADVENTURES.

JULES, THE WISE OLD OCTOPUS, APPEARED
AND CALLED OUT TO NARAH AS SHE WAS SWIMMING AWAY.

"WHY DO YOU HIDE THIS GIFT?" JULES ASKED.

NARAH REPLIED, "I TREASURE HIS FRIENDSHIP,
SO I PUT IT IN A TREASURE CHEST."

JULES EXPLAINED, "THIS IS NOT A GIFT LIKE GOLD OR SILVER.
THIS IS A GIFT TO MAKE THE WORLD A BETTER PLACE.
YOU WERE BORN DIFFERENT FOR A REASON.
NOW USE THAT REASON FOR GOOD."

NARAH STILL DOUBTED HERSELF.

JULES CONTINUED TO TEACH, "I HEARD YOUR SPEECH FOR PEG. YOU DON'T THINK THAT APPLIES TO YOU?"

NARAH SHRUGGED HER FINS.

SO JULES HAD TO PROVE IT TO HER. HE PLACED THE HORN IN NARAH'S BARNACLE. A PERFECT FIT.

THE WISE OLD OCTOPUS LEFT HER WITH ONE LAST THOUGHT...

"WHY BE A WHALE WHEN YOU CAN BE A NARAH WHALE?"

HE WRAPPED ALL EIGHT ARMS AROUND HER AND PROCLAIMED, "FROM THIS DAY FORWARD... YOU WILL BE A KNOWN AS THE NARWHAL."

One clear morning,
Narah saw a turtle
stuck in a fishing net.

On that day,
she finally realized why Peg
left her such an amazing gift.

She sliced through the ropes like a sword and freed the trapped sea turtle.

ONE CHILLY AFTERNOON,
A BABY SEAL WAS STRANDED UNDER THE ICE.

WITH ALL HER MIGHT,
NARAH RAMMED THROUGH THE GLACIER
AND CREATED A PASSAGE TO SAFETY
FOR THE SCARED SEAL.

ONE STORMY NIGHT,
A PIRATE SHIP LOST ITS WAY
IN A THICK AND FOREBODING FOG.

NARAH FOUND AN OIL LANTERN
AND HUNG IT FROM THE TOP OF HER HORN.
SHE GUIDED THE ENTIRE CREW TO DRY LAND.

STILL TO THIS DAY,
EVERY TIME THE SUN GOES DOWN
AND THE MOON RISES UP,
NARAH WAVES AND THANKS HER FRIEND IN THE SKY
FOR THE PRECIOUS GIFT.

PEG LOOKS OVER NARAH FROM THE STARS ABOVE.
HE DOESN'T HAVE A HORN ANYMORE...
HE'S SPROUTED ANGEL WINGS.

There are no more Unicorns in this world...
All we have left are the Narwhals.

A portion of proceeds from this book
will go to helping Narah and her friends
from becoming endangered. #narahthewhale